Be Patient, Little Chick

Claude Clément
Adapted by Patricia Jensen
Illustrations by Erost

Reader's Digest Kids
Pleasantville, N.Y.— Montreal

One bright spring day, a hen's egg began to crack open. After a short while, a little chick burst out, looking in wonder at the world around him.

Still wearing part of his shell, the impatient chick decided it was time to get up and explore the world.

"Which way is the garden?" he asked his mother. "Where are the great woods?"

"Now, now, Little Chick," said Mama gently. "You've been part of this world only a short time. You shouldn't be in such a hurry to grow up. Good things come to those who wait."

"What kinds of things?" asked Little Chick, taking a peek at the farmyard.

"You shall see when the time comes," said Mama. "Right now you are still a very little chick. Someday soon you will see the garden and the woods, but before that time, there are many things you need to learn."

"I already know everything I need to know," said Little Chick confidently.

"Is that so?" said Mama. "Well, the most important thing for you to learn is to stay close by me while you are still small. That way I can protect you."

"I can take care of myself," declared Little Chick, hurrying out into the farmyard.

Suddenly, he was surrounded by some large turkeys.

"Maybe I should stick by Mama," said Little Chick to himself nervously. "She might get scared all by herself!"

Little Chick rushed back to his mother.

"I thought you might find it a little frightening out on your own," she said. "Have some grain before one of those turkeys decides he wants it."

Little Chick looked at the ground in disgust. "Grain!" he grumbled. "I would much rather eat other things!"

Little Chick spotted a small dog bone and walked over to it. He pecked and pecked, but no matter how hard he tried, he couldn't eat it.

"Grain is the best thing for little chicks to eat," said Mama softly. "You will be able to eat other things when you are older. Now come back with me and eat your breakfast with the rest of the chicks."

"All right," said Little Chick. "But when I get bigger, I'm going to eat dog bones every single day!"

Mama laughed as she nudged Little Chick back to breakfast. But no sooner had he begun to eat than something else caught his attention.

"Look at that bird!" Little Chick cried. "Oh, Mama, it looks so beautiful up there!"

Little Chick dashed after the bird. "Wait for me!" he shouted, flapping his wings. "I want to fly with you!"

"Little Chick!" called Mama. "Come back here! Chicks can't fly like that bird."

"I bet I'll be able to fly like that when I get bigger," said Little Chick stubbornly.

Mama smiled as she led the spunky chick back to the farmyard.

"Now please stay here, where I can keep an eye on you," she told Little Chick.

But Little Chick was still impatient. The moment Mama wasn't looking, he ran down to the pond.

"I'll join you for a swim," Little Chick called to a duck in the pond.

"Chicks can't swim!" said the duck. Little Chick was about to protest when he heard the familiar clucking of his mother. Before she could catch him, he ran off.

Little Chick ran so fast that he bumped into the biggest of the roosters.

"Watch where you're going!" shouted the rooster.

"You don't scare me," Little Chick shouted back in his loudest voice.

"You need someone to teach you a lesson," crowed the rooster. He strutted toward the chick.

"Help me!" cried Little Chick. "Mama! Mama! Help!"

Quick as could be, Mama came running. She cackled loudly, ruffled her feathers, and flapped her wings at the rooster.

Little Chick hid behind a bush, safe from the angry rooster.

"I hope Mama doesn't get hurt," he whispered fearfully.

Mama cackled and flapped her wings until, finally, the rooster trotted off in a huff.

Back in their nest, Little Chick cuddled up very close to Mama.

"Be patient, Little Chick," she said. "Before you know it, you'll be one of the biggest roosters in the farmyard and ready to see the great, wide world. But it takes time to grow up and learn all the things you need to learn. Remember this—good things come to those who wait."

"I'm not in such a hurry anymore, Mama," said Little Chick. "I'll stay close to you until I get a little bigger." Then he nestled under his mother's wing, snug and warm, safe and sound.

Before a chick is born, it grows inside an egg for 21 days. The mother hen keeps the egg warm by sitting on it.

A chick's first feathers are called *down*. When a chick cracks through the shell of an egg, the chick is all wet. Then its down begins to dry and fluff out.

The mother hen shows the chick what is good to eat. Chicks know how to peck at food as soon as they are born.